3-Minute Take-Along Treasury

Animal Stories

CONTENTS

sequoia™
children's publishing

Counting Sheep

Written by Catherine McCafferty
Illustrated by Kathy Wilburn

Fleecy was a young lamb who was full of energy. She romped through the meadows every day. She could run and play all day long.

The crickets and butterflies let her chase them through the fields. None of the other sheep could keep up with the little insects. But pouncing, prancing Fleecy surely could. She never wore out.

At the end of the day, Fleecy's friends would fly away. Fleecy wished she could fly like the crickets and butterflies. She thought of the sky as a wonderful magical place. Fleecy spent each night staring at it. Fleecy believed that someday she might fly.

The lively little lamb got so wrapped up in her thoughts some nights, she was just about ready to jump right out of her fleece and up to the stars. Fleecy had so much energy that she stayed awake even when it was time to sleep.

Fleecy's mother began to worry about her. "It's not good for a little lamb to stay up so late," her mother told her one night. "A growing lamb needs her sleep."

"I'd like to dream and be awake at the same time, Mom," Fleecy said.

Fleecy's mother had an idea. She knew of Fleecy's fondness for the sky. "Look up to the sky," she said, "and count the stars you see. I'm sure you'll fall asleep soon."

Fleecy gazed up at the bright stars in the night sky. She imagined she was high above the field, flying among them. In her dream, she sailed from star to brilliant star, tapping each one as she counted it.

"One, two, three," Fleecy counted. She only got to three before she slipped into sleep.

Fleecy's mother was right. Fleecy slept so well that the next day she had more energy than ever.

"I flew higher than a butterfly in my dream last night," she told her friends as she chased butterflies through the field. "I even touched the stars!"

That night, when it was time for bed, there were no stars to count. Fleecy was very disappointed. She hoped to fly in her dreams and touch many more stars this time.

Again, Fleecy could not sleep. Even after a busy day with the butterflies, Fleecy was still full of energy.

Fleecy's mother had a good idea. "Try counting the clouds tonight, dear," she said.

Fleecy watched the clouds slowly crossing the night sky. In her mind, she jumped from cloud to cloud. To Fleecy, every cloud was a soft, cool pillow that wrapped gently around her.

"One, two, three," she counted before she was fast asleep.

The next morning, Fleecy was full of energy again.

"Last night I hopped from cloud to cloud," Fleecy told her mother.

"I'm so glad you slept well," Fleecy's mother said.

"I sure did!" Fleecy said as she ran through a field.

"Have fun playing with your friends!" Fleecy's mother said.

After another busy day, it was bedtime once again. But that night there were no clouds or stars.

"How will I get to sleep now?" Fleecy asked her mother.

Fleecy's mother thought for a moment. Then she said, "Try counting the sheep. We will always be here."

"I'll try," Fleecy said.

Fleecy started counting all the sheep sleeping in the field. She imagined that she floated high above the field, and the sleeping sheep rose up with her as she counted them. In her mind, every sheep's woolly coat was a puffy cloud in the dark sky.

"One, two, three," she counted as she floated.

Fleecy only got to three before she was sleeping soundly, just like the rest of the sheep.

From then on, Fleecy's mother never had to worry about her restlessness. That is because Fleecy counted sheep every night.

Though she tried again and again, Fleecy was never able to fly like her friends in the meadow did. But in her starry dreams she came closer to flying than any little lamb had ever known.

Baby Bluebird

Written by Lisa Harkrader
Illustrated by Cristina Ong

Baby Bluebird looked up at the sky. She watched all the other birds flying. "It's spring," she said. "I should be flying, but I don't know how to start."

Her friend Rabbit watched the birds, too.

"Flying looks a lot like hopping," said Rabbit. "In fact, I see birds hopping about all the time. Practice hopping with me. If you hop high enough, you might start to fly."

Rabbit hopped off through the garden. Baby Bluebird hopped after her. She was in the air, but soon came back down to the ground. Baby Bluebird tried again and again.

"What do you think, Baby Bluebird?" asked Rabbit. "Is hopping like flying?"

"It's a little like flying," she said. "But I keep landing. I don't think real flying is so bouncy."

Baby Bluebird sat down in the pasture. She watched the other birds as they hopped and lifted off the ground.

Her friend Turtle watched the birds, too.

"Flying looks a little like swimming," he said. "Maybe if you practice swimming through the water with me, it will help you learn to glide through the air when you fly."

Baby Bluebird watched Turtle glide around the farm pond. "That doesn't look so hard," she said.

She plunged into the water. "It's so wet!" she cried.

"Paddle out here to the middle," said Turtle.

Baby Bluebird tried to paddle. She splashed and sputtered and glugged. Baby Bluebird wanted to glide like Turtle. But she could not.

"Maybe swimming isn't like flying after all," she said. "I don't think flying is so soggy."

Baby Bluebird pulled herself on to the grassy edge of the pond. She fluttered her wings to dry them.

When her wings were dry, Baby Bluebird went to the farmhouse and found Cat and Dog curled up on the porch. Baby Bluebird sat down beside them and watched the birds flying above her.

The birds playfully swooped through the sky. As they flew, they even sang a pretty song.

"These birds can fly *and* sing," said Baby Bluebird.

Cat and Dog watched and heard the birds, too.

"Maybe singing is part of flying," said Cat. "If you sing loud enough and long enough, maybe you'll begin to fly, too. We'll help you."

Dog howled. Cat yowled. Baby Bluebird tweeted. Then she twittered. She took a deep breath and let out a squawk!

But nobody started to fly. Not Dog. Not Cat. Not even Baby Bluebird.

"It's no use," said Baby Bluebird. "Singing won't make me fly. I might as well stop trying."

Baby Bluebird

"Thank goodness," said Dog. "I don't have any howls left."

"Stop trying?" said Cat. "You can't stop trying. If you want to fly, you must find a way."

Baby Bluebird sat down on the porch steps and put her head in her wings. Suddenly, she looked up.

"Singing was not enough. And neither was hopping or gliding," she said. "But now I think I know what I need to do to fly."

Baby Bluebird took a running start. She hopped like Rabbit. Once she was in the air, she glided like Turtle and the other birds through the beautiful sky.

"I'm flying!" she chirped.

Baby Bluebird swooped through the clouds. She flitted from tree to tree. Then Baby Bluebird lifted her head and, like Cat and Dog, began to sing.

Bridget's New Look

Written by Lisa Harkrader
Illustrated by Elena Kucharik

Lucy Ladybug rushed around her beauty shop getting ready for her customers. "Everyone in town will be here today. They want to look nice for the ball tonight."

Lucy's customers always asked for exactly what they wanted, and Lucy always made sure she gave them exactly what they asked for. Lucy made sure she had everything she would need.

"Lavender shampoo for Hannah Honeybee," said Lucy. "Christine Cricket's styling gel. And extra-firm hair spray for Greta Grasshopper."

Lucy lined up the bottles and unlocked the door of Lucy's Beauty Shop. Hannah, Christine, and Greta hurried through the doors.

Hannah pointed to a picture in a magazine. "Can you make my hair look like this?" she asked.

"Of course," Lucy said.

"My hair needs to be washed and curled," said Christine. "I know exactly how I want it curled, too."

"Have a seat," said Lucy.

"Can you trim an inch off my hair?" asked Greta.

"No problem," Lucy said.

Then Lucy quickly went to work.

Lucy washed and rolled Christine's hair. Then she cut Hannah's bangs. While Christine sat under the hair dryer, she trimmed an inch off Greta's hair.

Soon Christine's hair was dry. Lucy unrolled it. Then she combed it until it shined.

"Exactly what I wanted," said Christine.

Lucy sprayed Greta's hair with hair spray. Then she tied it back with a bow.

"You always give me exactly what I ask for," said Greta.

Lucy pinned Hannah's hair up onto her head. "Here is your new style," said Lucy. "It's called a beehive."

"Perfect!" said Hannah.

As Christine, Greta, and Hannah admired their hairstyles in the mirror, Betty Beetle hurried into Lucy's Beauty Shop with her daughter, Bridget. They both needed their hair styled for the ball, too.

Lucy set to work.

"How wonderful!" exclaimed Betty when Lucy was finally finished. "You always give me exactly what I want."

Bridget had been very quiet. "What kind of style do you want?" Lucy asked her.

Bridget shrugged. She knew what to do on a pitcher's mound or in a batter's box, but she had never been to Lucy's shop before.

"Something nice," said Bridget.
"Something nice it is," said Lucy.

Lucy trimmed and curled Bridget's hair. Her hair sprang up in coils all over her head.

"Adorable!" said Hannah Honeybee.

But Bridget did not say anything. She just sat very still in her chair.

"Is it what you wanted?" asked Lucy.

Bridget stared down at her sneakers. "Well, not exactly," she mumbled.

"Let's try again," said Lucy.

She combed, teased, and sprayed Bridget's hair. Then she handed Bridget a mirror.

"Beautiful," said Bridget's mother.

"This isn't what you wanted, either, is it?" asked Lucy.

"I really like ponytails," Bridget finally said.

Lucy pulled Bridget's hair back into two ponytails and tied a pink ribbon around each one.

Bridget looked in the mirror. "This is exactly what I wanted!" she said happily.

Lucy nodded. "Here at Lucy's Beauty Shop, when you ask for what you want, you get what you ask for."

"It looks wonderful!" said Bridget's mother.

"Thank you for making my hair so pretty," Bridget said as she looked in the mirror.

Lucy waved good-bye to her customers. Then she looked at her watch. "I need to hurry if I'm going to fix my hair in time for the ball."

The ball was lovely! Everyone looked gorgeous, and it was all thanks to Lucy!

Baby Pig

Written by Lenaya Raack
Illustrated by Kathy Rusynyk

A young girl kneels in the hay and watches Mother Pig feed her new litter of piglets. The little girl gets up and quietly moves around to the other side.

The pigs are all perfectly pink—except for the littlest one on the end. She has brown spots all over her body. This is the little girl's favorite piglet. She calls her Baby Pig.

Baby Pig moves with her family to a new home. It is called a sty or pigpen. It has a fence around it and lots of hay on the ground. Baby Pig lives there with Mother and Father Pig and her sisters and brothers. At night, the piglets sleep very close together to stay warm. Sometimes they even sleep on top of one another.

Today, Baby Pig wakes up first. She sniffs the ground looking for food. She is hungry all the time.

Then Baby Pig hears the girl coming. Baby Pig watches her pour the food into a long wooden bucket called a trough. Now all the pigs are awake. Baby Pig has to push past the other hungry pigs to eat.

It is summertime on the farm and it is hot. The ground is dry and dusty. The chickens roll in the dust to keep their feathers from sticking together. Baby Pig does not sweat, so she needs to roll in the mud to get cool.

Soon the girl brings out a hose, and makes a big mud hole by spraying cool water on the dirt. Baby Pig is the first one to jump in the mud. She rolls and wiggles and splashes until she is covered in mud. She is not hot anymore. The other pigs follow Baby Pig. They run and jump into the mud, too. Soon all the pigs are the color of mud. The little girl laughs. "I can hardly see you in all that mud," she says.

Sometimes the girl takes Baby Pig for walks. Today they are going for a walk down the road. Baby Pig likes to go for walks because there are lots of new things for her to see. She watches a squirrel run up a tree and a rabbit hop into a bush. Baby Pig stops to smell the yellow flowers that grow along the road. As they walk a little farther up the road, they see dogs herding a large flock of sheep. Baby Pig wants to help. The girl reminds Baby Pig that pigs do not herd sheep.

Then they stop under an apple tree to rest. The girl feeds Baby Pig an apple for being so good.

Baby Pig is hungry again. This time, Baby Pig tries the corn growing in the field. She squeezes under the fence and races for the big cornstalks. Baby Pig knocks over a cornstalk and eats the ears of corn.

The corn is too tall! Baby Pig cannot see the barnyard.

Then Baby Pig hears a familiar voice. It is the girl! Baby Pig squeals and the girl comes running to find her.

Baby Pig

Baby Pig is five months old now. She is too big for the little girl to pick up. But Baby Pig likes to follow the girl around the barnyard while the girl does all of her chores. She watches as the girl throws grain onto the ground and all of the chickens gobble it up.

The farm is quiet. It is nighttime now. In the barn, the cows sleepily eat one last mouthful of hay. The calves are already asleep in their stalls. The hens are sitting on their nests in the henhouse. Their chicks are safely tucked under their mothers' feathers. Outside, the pigs are back in their sty. They are lying down and getting ready to sleep, too.

The barnyard is dark and empty now. The farmhouse is quiet. Baby Pig and the girl sit on the bottom step of the front porch. They watch the fireflies blinking on and off in the darkness.

When it is time for bed, the girl walks Baby Pig back to her pen and gives her a good-night hug.

Baby Penguin

Written by Jennifer Boudart
Illustrated by Lori Nelson Field

Ark! Ark! At the frozen seaside, the penguins greet each other with a loud barking noise. Father Penguin returns from a swim in the sea. He builds up speed until he can leap out of the water and land on the ice. Then he shakes the water off his feathers. It is Father Penguin's turn to stay close to the nest so Mother Penguin can go fishing.

Mother Penguin climbs from the nest. Her movements wake her baby. Baby Penguin blinks her bright black eyes.

Baby Penguin is a slowpoke. When she was born, she took half a day to break out of her shell. It takes a long time for her to eat, too. And even though she is three weeks old, she has never left her nest.

Penguins are everywhere. They are all squawking loudly! They sure are noisy.

Penguins are birds, but they cannot fly. Baby Penguin's wings are really more like flippers. Although she will never fly in the sky like other birds, Baby Penguin will be able to fly through the water with her special wings.

The penguin family guards its nest. If a stranger gets too close, Father Penguin stretches his neck. His neck feathers fluff out. He points his head up to the sky and grunts.

Baby Penguin stretches her neck and grunts, too. Father Penguin and his baby tell the stranger to keep away from their home.

Father Penguin protected Baby Penguin when she was just an egg, too. He held the egg on top of his feet so it would not touch the ice for almost two months. A flap of warm belly skin covered the egg and kept it warm. Baby Penguin is lucky to have Father Penguin!

Mother and Father Penguin must go fishing often to catch enough food for their tiny baby. They will have to leave her for a while. Baby Penguin's mother and father bring her to a group of young penguins. She slowly waddles after them.

Baby Penguin will be safe in this group. All of the older penguins will watch for danger. They circle around the babies and shelter them from cold winds.

Soon Mother and Father Penguin will teach her how to swim really fast through the water, away from danger.

Baby Penguin is very hungry. Suddenly, she hears her father calling to her! Will he find her? Baby Penguin is lost in a crowd of fuzzy little black penguins that look just like her.

Baby Penguin lifts her head and barks as loudly as she can. Her parents hear her over all the other noise. They find her!

Baby Penguin is happy to return to the nest with Mother and Father Penguin. She knows it is time for them to feed her the fish that they have caught in the sea.

Penguins get all of their food from the ocean. They eat fish, crab, and squid. When penguins get thirsty, they can eat snow to quench their thirst.

Penguins have bodies that are built for the coldest weather on earth. They have warm feathers and a thick layer of fat all over their bodies to keep them warm.

Baby Penguin

A few weeks have passed. Baby Penguin has new feathers. She looks like a grown-up. Baby Penguin flaps her flippers. The penguins form a big group near the water.

Baby Penguin follows them. She uses her flippers to slide across the cold ice on her belly.

Baby Penguin quickly discovers that sliding is the best way to get around on the cold snow and ice.

It is now time for the young penguins' first swim in the sea. Baby Penguin is one of the last little penguins to dive into the water. She swims really fast! Baby Penguin is no longer such a slowpoke!

Bear Cub

Written by Sarah Toast
Illustrated by Krista Brauckmann-Towns

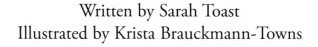

As summer draws to an end, Mother Bear roams through the forest, gathering and eating enormous amounts of berries and fruit.

Mother Bear is putting on fat so she will stay very warm in her den all winter long.

The extra fat will also help her provide rich milk for the baby bear that will be born.

Mother Bear chooses a rocky cave to be her den during the winter. Inside the den, she and her baby will be protected from the cold wind and blowing snow.

In the middle of winter, when the snowdrifts are deep outside the den, Mother Bear's cub is born. With closed eyes and hardly any fur, the little cub will grow very quickly, nourished by Mother Bear's rich milk.

Bear Cub and Mother Bear sleep on, but Mother Bear will protect her cub if their winter home is disturbed.

In a few weeks, Bear Cub's eyes open. He is now covered in thick soft fur.

Bear cubs will stay in their mother's den for three months before they venture outside. During these three months, they spend most of their time sleeping. The cubs wake only to drink their mother's milk.

In the spring, Bear Cub and his mother emerge from the warm winter den.

Mother Bear shows Bear Cub how to look through the forest for tender shoots that will make a good meal.

They make their way down a grassy slope to the elks' winter range. They lift up their heads and sniff the breeze.

Bear Cub

Mother Bear finds an elk that died in the winter. Mother Bear eats as much as she can of the nourishing meat. Then she carefully buries it in a shallow hole.

Bear Cub learns by watching what his mother does. The most important rules for Bear Cub are to follow Mother, obey Mother, and have fun.

Bear cubs stay with their mother for about two years. When his mother stops to rest, Bear Cub likes to play. He climbs all over her. He somersaults into her lap and nibbles her ears. Then he runs off to chase a tiny field mouse.

The bear cub also learns many survival tips from his mother, such as what to eat and how to escape danger, before he ventures out on his own.

Mother Bear teaches her baby cub to turn over fallen branches and look for grubs to eat. With their sharp claws, Bear Cub and Mother Bear dig up bulbs, roots, and snails.

Bears will eat almost anything they can get their paws on, including grasses, berries, tree bark, plants, insects, some small mammals, and sweet honey!

Bear Cub

Bear Cub has found a treat. It is a honeycomb with honey from last summer still inside. Bear Cub sticks his little paw in the honeycomb and then licks it. He tastes the wildflowers of summer in the sweet honey.

As Bear Cub's first summer draws to an end, he is able to find his own food, although he might drink milk from Mother Bear occasionally. Now he must eat as much food as he can to prepare for his long winter sleep.

Clover's Patch

Written by Catherine McCafferty
Illustrated by Erin Mauterer

Clover was a little calf. She lived with some other cows and calves on a farm. The farm had a big pasture with plenty of sweet green grass to eat.

There was so much grassy land that all of the cows had their own eating spots. Clover's favorite place was the patch of grass by the big gray rock.

"This must be the sweetest grass in the field," she thought.

A little ground squirrel lived in a burrow under the gray rock. He did not like Clover eating so close to his home, because he did not like the sound of her bell. It clanged whenever Clover strolled from one tuft of grass to another. The ground squirrel covered his ears, but it never helped.

One day, the ground squirrel thought of a plan. "How do you know that the grass by the gray rock is the sweetest grass in the pasture?" he asked Clover.

"I know that I really like this grass," she said. "And this is my favorite spot in the whole field."

The ground squirrel thought for a minute. "Let me tell you a little secret," he whispered. "I have heard that the grass on the hillside is really the best-tasting grass of all."

Clover looked at the hillside, where another calf, Daisy, was eating at her favorite spot. Daisy looked very happy munching on some posies.

"You should try that grass," the ground squirrel said.

"Her grass does look greener and sweeter," said Clover. "I think I'll pay her a visit."

Clover walked over to Daisy.

"Hello," she said. "May I have a nibble of your grass?"

"Of course," said Daisy.

Clover had a nibble and smiled. The grass seemed so good that Clover took another bite, then another and another. Soon Clover helped herself to all of the grass.

"That ground squirrel was right," said Clover. "This grass is better."

Clover kept on eating, which did not make Daisy happy.

But what could Daisy do? She wanted to share, but did not want Clover to eat all of her grass.

Finally, Clover took a break from eating and looked up. She saw Lily eating in her favorite spot by the fence. Lily looked really happy. Her grass also looked greener and sweeter than Daisy's.

"I wonder if Lily's grass is sweeter than this grass," Clover. said. She took one final nibble.

"I think I'll pay Lily a visit," Clover said. "I'll ask her if I can taste her grass."

Clover trotted over to the fence where Lily ate. "Hello, Lily," she said. "May I have a nibble of your grass?"

"Sure," said Lily.

Clover had a nibble and grinned from ear to ear. The grass seemed so very sweet that Clover took another bite, then another and another. Soon Clover helped herself to all the grass in sight!

"This grass seems even better than Daisy's," said Clover. "This grass is the best-tasting grass of all."

Clover kept on eating, which did not make Lily happy. But Lily knew just what to do.

Lily left Clover by the fence. She went to find Sweetheart, the wisest cow in the field.

Lily walked to Sweetheart's favorite spot on the other side of the pasture. Sure enough, Lily found Sweetheart. Her friend Daisy was there, too!

"It's so nice to see the both of you on this fine day," said Sweetheart. "What brings you here for a visit?"

"I hope you can help me," said Daisy. "I was eating the grass on the hillside, when Clover came over and ate and ate and ate."

53

"Then she came over to my patch," said Lily. "And she's eating there now."

"I think I know the problem," said Sweetheart. "Clover doesn't know that the grass in her patch is just as sweet and good as any grass in the pasture."

Sweetheart found Clover still eating at Lily's patch.

"Would you like to taste the sweetest grass in the field?" Sweetheart asked kindly.

"Oh, yes!" said Clover.

"Well, close your eyes, dear, and I'll lead you to it."

Clover and Sweetheart walked for a bit. Then Sweetheart said, "This is the place."

Clover kept her eyes closed and munched the grass where she stood. "This grass is so-o-o delicious!" said Clover.

"This is your own patch," said Sweetheart.

Clover saw that it was her favorite spot by the gray rock.

The ground squirrel hurried out of his burrow. He had been lonely without Clover. "I heard the grass by the gray rock is the sweetest grass in the pasture," he said.

The Four Musicians

Adapted by Lynne Suesse
Illustrated by Melissa Iwai

An old donkey lives in a big green pasture. The donkey loves working for the farmer and pulling the farmer's cart to and from town.

Sometimes the donkey's back gets sore and the loads seem to get heavier and heavier. But the donkey is happy to be needed by the farmer.

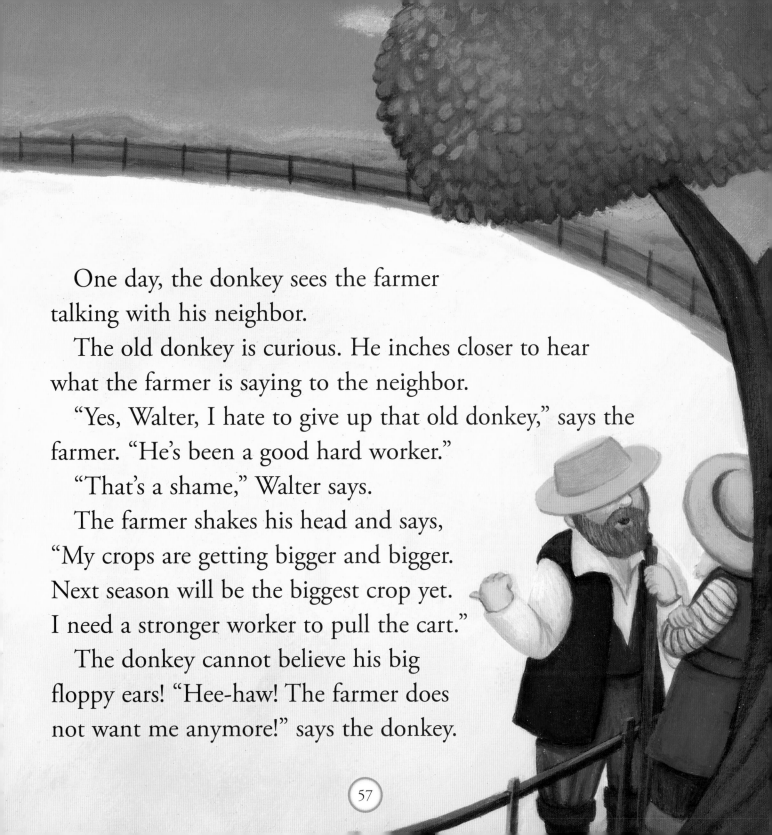

One day, the donkey sees the farmer talking with his neighbor.

The old donkey is curious. He inches closer to hear what the farmer is saying to the neighbor.

"Yes, Walter, I hate to give up that old donkey," says the farmer. "He's been a good hard worker."

"That's a shame," Walter says.

The farmer shakes his head and says, "My crops are getting bigger and bigger. Next season will be the biggest crop yet. I need a stronger worker to pull the cart."

The donkey cannot believe his big floppy ears! "Hee-haw! The farmer does not want me anymore!" says the donkey.

The donkey is very sad. The donkey loves to sing. So he decides right there that he will move to the town of Bremen to become a musician.

On his way to Bremen, the donkey meets a sad dog.

"What is wrong?" asks the donkey.

"My master says I am too old to hunt," says the dog.

The donkey asks the dog to become a musician.

"Bow-wow! I'm a great singer," says the dog.

Soon they meet another sad face. It is a cat.

"My master thinks I'm too old to catch mice," says the cat.

The dog and the donkey quickly invite the cat to join their musical group in Bremen. The donkey, the dog, and the cat practice singing as they walk down the road to Bremen.

Soon they see something in the road. It is the rooster from the dairy farm. The rooster does not look happy.

"The farmer bought a new alarm clock," says the rooster. "He says he does not need an old rooster like me anymore."

The donkey, the dog, and the cat tell the rooster about their plan to become musicians.

"Cock-a-doodle-doo! I can sing, too!" crows the rooster.

Now the donkey, the dog, the cat, and the rooster make their way to the town of Bremen.

The four friends walk until nighttime. They are very tired. As they stop to rest, the donkey sees a bright light far off in the distance.

The dog, the cat, and the rooster listen closely to the donkey. The donkey tells them that they can get food and a place to sleep at the house. They can sing for the people who live there, like proper musicians!

The four friends walk up to the house. They stand outside the window, one on top of the other, and get ready to sing.

Inside the house, they see some men counting piles of money. The men have lots of good food to eat.

The four musicians know that they must sing as loudly as they possibly can to get some tasty food. They open their mouths and sing, "Cock-a-doodle-doo! Hee-haw! Meow! Bow-wow!"

The men inside the house jump out of their seats. They look out the window and see a four-headed beast making a terrible noise!

The men are robbers, and they think that the four-headed beast is punishing them for stealing.

Quickly, the men run from the house. They do not look back as they head into the woods.

The donkey, the dog, the cat, and the rooster are surprised when the men leave in such a hurry.

"They must be going to get more people to hear our music," says the donkey. "We should make ourselves right at home. We want to be rested for our next performance."

The donkey, the dog, the cat, and the rooster settle into the house. They have a big wonderful meal. They each go to bed with a full tummy.

The robbers never do come back to the house. But the four musicians sing every day, just in case.

Little Squeak

Written by Sarah Toast
Illustrated by Richard Bernal

Once there was a small mouse named Little Squeak who lived in a great big house. She had a very nice cozy mouse hole in a corner of the children's playroom.

Little Squeak loved to sit quietly in the doorway of her mouse hole and watch the little boy and girl play with all their toys.

One night, Little Squeak decided to have a closer look at the children's wonderful toys. Little Squeak waited patiently until the little children were tucked into bed and fast

asleep. Then she quietly crept into their playroom.

At that moment, the moon shone in through the window, lighting up the room and bringing all the toys to life.

"Come and play with us, Little Squeak!" called the toys.

Little Squeak was so excited. But she did not know where to begin.

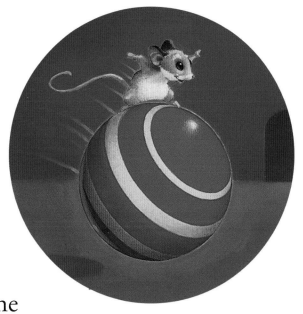

"Little Squeak, come play with me!" cried the red rubber ball. "I can bounce and bounce all over the playroom!"

Little Squeak jumped on top of the ball and rode it around the room.

"Boing, boing!" went the ball. It was very exciting. But after a little while, all of the bouncing began to make Little Squeak dizzy.

"Thank you, but I'm looking for something a little less bouncy," said Little Squeak politely.

Little Squeak hopped off the ball and scurried over to the toy chest. She peeked inside and found a big robot.

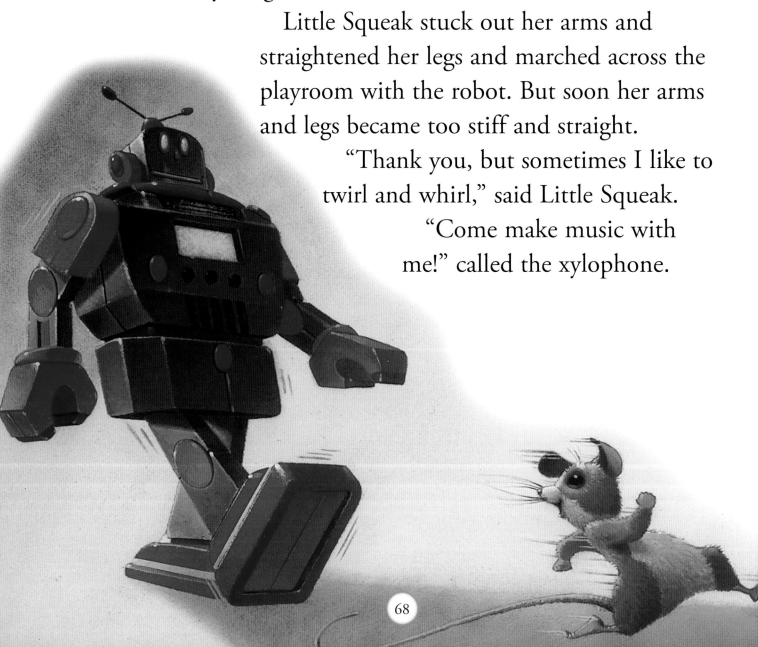

"Come march with me, Little Squeak!" said the bright blue robot as he climbed out of the toy chest. "I can clang and clatter all day long!"

Little Squeak stuck out her arms and straightened her legs and marched across the playroom with the robot. But soon her arms and legs became too stiff and straight.

"Thank you, but sometimes I like to twirl and whirl," said Little Squeak.

"Come make music with me!" called the xylophone.

68

Little Squeak hopped up onto the xylophone. Soon Little Squeak was whirling and twirling, and dancing all over the colorful keys.

Little Squeak hummed and sang while the xylophone played along. What a lovely tune they made! Little Squeak loved music.

But after a while, Little Squeak's tiny feet began to get tired.

"I need a rest!" said Little Squeak.

Just then, the toy bug zoomed up beside her.

"Come along for a ride with me, Little Squeak!" said the toy bug.

After a wild ride, the toy bug skidded to a stop right in front of the airplane hangar.

"Thank you, but I'm looking for something a little less bumpy," said Little Squeak.

Little Squeak heard a loud buzz and a whir. The noises came from inside the toy airplane hangar.

"Why don't you come fly with me?" said the shiny new jet.

The jet puttered out of the airplane hangar. Little Squeak climbed into the pilot's seat.

Just then, Little Squeak heard someone coming up the stairs. The children had finished breakfast, and they were coming up to say good morning to their toys.

Little Squeak

"Time to go home," said Little Squeak. The jet plane landed right beside Little Squeak's front door. Little Squeak hurried back into her hole.

"I hope all of our toys do not get lonely while we are sleeping," the little boy said.

"Don't worry!" Little Squeak whispered. "Your toys will never be lonely with me around."

Dabble Duckling

Written by Sarah Toast
Illustrated by Judith Love

It is summer, and Mother Duck is making a nest. In a clump of reeds near the edge of the pond, Mother Duck finds a hollow place in the ground. She lines it with grass and soft cattail stems.

Mother Duck lays her nine smooth eggs. She plucks soft feathers from her breast to line the nest and protect the eggs.

Mother Duck sits on her eggs for many days and nights. Whenever she leaves the nest, she covers her eggs with a soft blanket of down to hide them and keep them warm.

At last, Mother Duck hears her ducklings working to get out of their shells. The last little duckling to break out of its shell is called Dabble.

The ducklings will stay very close to their mother until they can fly. It usually takes about two months before they learn to fly.

Dabble tries to stay very close to Mother Duck. She sees Mother Duck taking very good care of all of her brothers and sisters. She knows that her mother will take very good care of her, too.

The tiny ducklings are only a few hours old, but they can run. They follow their mother down to the water's edge for their very first swim.

Ducklings can usually swim right after they are born. But they must wait for their mother to waterproof their feathers before they can take their first swim.

Mother Duck can waterproof the ducklings feathers by rubbing them with a special oil. The oil that she uses comes from a place near her tail. This oil helps the ducklings stay warm in the water.

Dabble is the very first young duckling to jump into the water after Mother Duck. Her sisters and brothers gleefully jump in after her. They bob on the water like balls of fluff.

What a glorious and fun pond! There is so much for a little duckling to see.

Suddenly, Dabble is dazzled by a dragonfly that lands on a nearby lily pad. A colorful butterfly grabs her attention next. Then she stares at a caterpillar on a cattail leaf. Dabble likes to gracefully swim through the tiny waves in the pond.

Now Dabble is getting quite hungry, and she knows exactly what to do. She tips up her tail and stretches her bill down to the muddy bottom of the pond to find plenty of plants, roots, and seeds.

There is plenty of food now, but in the winter ducks cannot find insects, seeds, or plants to eat. So every fall, they fly south. The weather is warm there, and they will find plenty of food.

Dabble enjoys dipping down to look for food underwater, then popping up again to see where Mother Duck is.

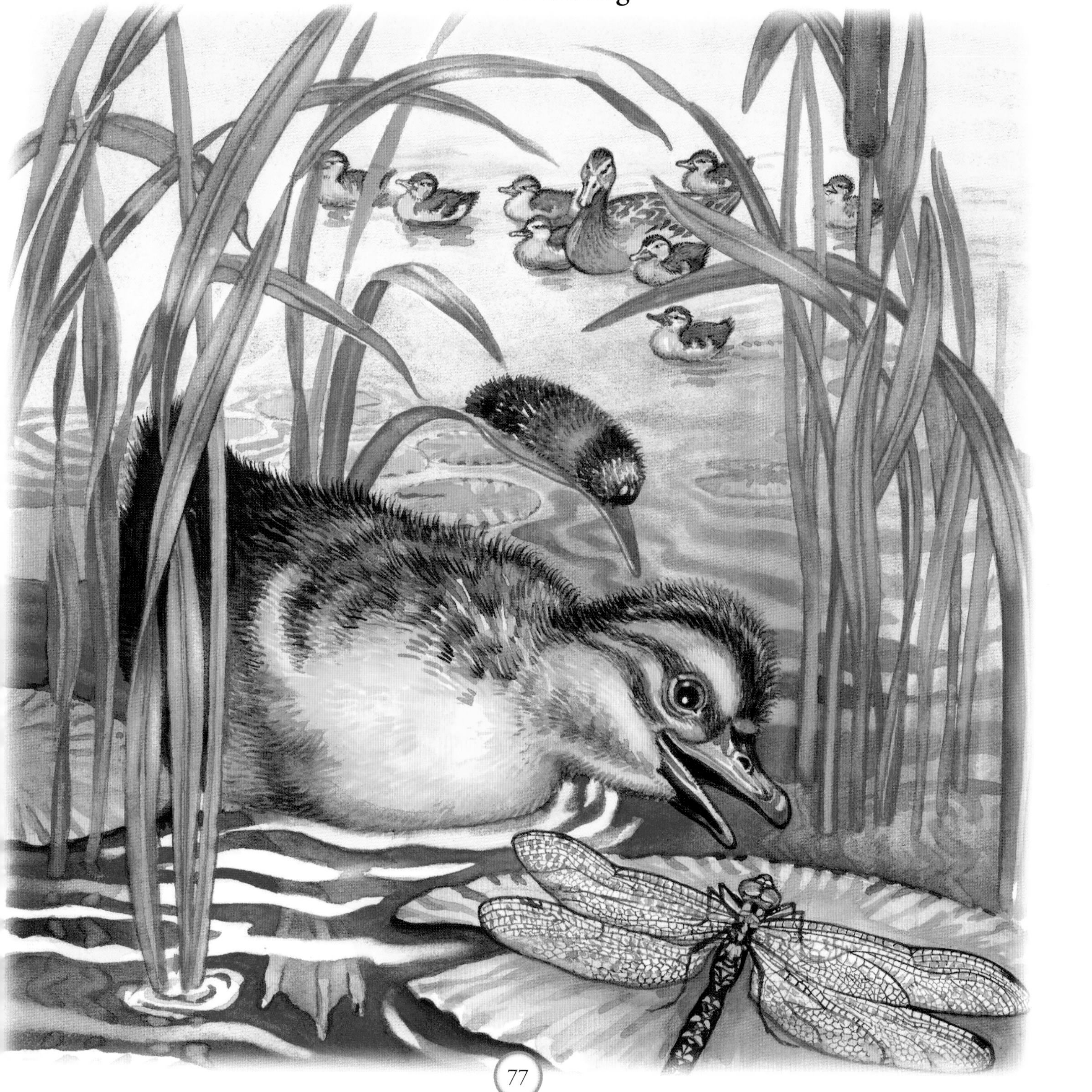

Dabbling is what Dabble does when she turns upside down to look for food underwater. Only her tail can be seen above the water.

Dabble watches a colorful butterfly flitting among the reeds in the pond. Then Dabble dips down to enjoy another nibble. She lifts her tiny head to quack "hello" to a red-winged blackbird.

After a fun day, Mother Duck leads her ducklings safely back to the nest. That night, all the ducklings sleep together in the nest after their busy first day in the world. Dabble dreams about tomorrow, when she will see the bright butterfly again.

Goat Kids

Written by Catherine McCafferty
Illustrated by Andrea Tachiera

Goat twins Billy and Nanny stand up in the hay as the farmer comes into the barn.

Today, the farmer pats Nanny and Billy. "You two will have to look after yourselves today," the farmer says. He leads their mother away. Mama Goat will care for a newborn lamb whose own mother cannot take care of it.

What will Billy and Nanny do today?

Billy likes to eat. Nanny likes to jump and climb. But they also like to stay together.

Billy and Nanny nibble happily from the hay bin. They have had their teeth since they were born. And that is a good thing since Billy likes to eat all the time.

Nanny ventures out into the barnyard. Suddenly, she sees that the shed roof is just the right height for climbing. Nanny hops onto a hay bale, then leans her front hooves against the shed and jumps up.

Soon Billy joins Nanny. Their sturdy hooves keep them sure-footed. Like all goats, they have very good balance.

Nanny and Billy look around the farm from the top of the shed roof. They like being up where they can see everything.

High places are good lookouts for goats. If goats think danger is coming, they spread out and climb to high places to spot it. Then they leap down to surprise any enemies.

Billy and Nanny do not see any danger. But they do see that the roof slopes right down into the farmer's backyard. Billy thinks he might find a snack there.

After climbing down the other side of the roof, Billy and Nanny both land right in the farmer's backyard.

Billy stops at the farmer's kitchen door. He climbs the three little steps to the back porch and waits for the farmer's wife to open the door.

Nanny climbs up the steps, then down again. She does this a few times, then goes to find a higher place to climb. When Nanny gets to the farmer's pickup truck, she jumps onto the hood and then onto the roof. She climbs just the way mountain goats do, as if she is jumping from one narrow ledge to another.

Suddenly, Billy sees the farmer.

"I have a much better place for you," says the kind farmer.

The farmer leads Billy and Nanny to a big field. The field is covered with bushes and thick brush.

Billy and Nanny see other goats are already munching on the heavy undergrowth. Billy cannot wait to start eating all the delicious food!

Billy's first feeding stop is a thick prickly bush. Billy expects the plant to be nice and tender, but his tough mouth feels prickles instead. If Billy's mother was with him, she would eat the toughest parts of the plant, and leave the most delicious and tender parts for Billy and Nanny.

Billy is so busy eating that he does not notice Nanny wandering off. With the other goats around, Nanny does not mind being a little farther away from Billy.

Nanny tries to run and leap in the field, but it is too crowded with all the other goats. At the far end of the field, Nanny sees a fence. She trots toward it. The fence does not look too high.

Nanny leaps and sails over the fence into a grassy field. Then she jumps back into the brushy field. Then back over the fence again. When Nanny has jumped enough, she settles down to munch grass in the field.

Nanny does not see the cows munching nearby. But then she hears a loud "Mooooooo!"

Nanny crouches low to the ground as heavy footsteps get closer. Nanny peeks up and sees a cow for the first time! Nanny is very scared!

Nanny runs and runs across the grassy field to get away from the big animal. But she is also far away from Billy and the other goats. Nanny tries to find a good lookout spot, but the field is flat and open.

Suddenly, Nanny sees her mother in the open field. A cute newborn lamb stands next to Mama Goat.

Goat Kids

At the end of the day, the farmer leads Nanny and her mother back toward the brushy field. In the field, Billy is as full as he can be.

The farmer leads all the goats back to the barn. It has been a busy day for all of them. Nanny and Billy settle down in the hay. Their mother joins them. The three of them curl up in the hay and sleep soundly all night long.

The next morning, Nanny and Billy find some large wooden blocks stacked next to a tree. They carefully climb up the blocks. From there, Nanny can see everything on the farm and Billy can munch on the tree's tender leaves. Now they can both do what they like best — together!

Farm Kitten

Written by Catherine McCafferty
Illustrated by Debbie Pinkney

Today is a very special day! In a warm quiet corner of the barn, Mama Cat nestles in the hay and gives birth to five kittens.

Even though their eyes are not open, the kittens use their sense of smell to find their favorite spot to nurse each time they eat. Nursing is important since Mama Cat's milk keeps the kittens from getting sick.

As the kittens get older, Mama Cat will teach them how to become mousers and help the farmer. Mousers catch mice and rats that eat the farmer's corn and grains.

Farm Kitten is two weeks old now. His eyes are open and he can hear. But Farm Kitten still stays close to Mama Cat.

Mama Cat leaves her kittens safe in the barn when she goes out to catch a mouse or a rat.

Mama Cat has caught a rat today. Back at the barn, she shows her kittens how she caught it. All of the kittens will need to hunt for themselves someday. Farm Kitten watches his mother very carefully.

Farm Kitten is four weeks old and ready to explore. He steps out from his soft bed of hay.

Farm Kitten hears a noise in one of the stalls. He jumps up on the stall divider and swings his tail sideways to keep his balance. In the stall, he sees a huge brown cow! What a big animal! He fluffs up the hair on his back and tail and hisses as loud as he can. The big cow just keeps chewing her hay. She is not scared of Farm Kitten.

Farm Kitten looks down from his high place. He stretches as far as he can toward the ground, then slides the rest of the way down the stall.

Farm Kitten's wagging tail has attracted one of the farm puppies. Even though Farm Kitten and the puppy are both baby animals, they have different body signals.

The puppy does not know that Farm Kitten wags his tail when he is angry and scared. Puppies wag their tails when they are happy.

When Farm Kitten raises his paw to swat the puppy away, the puppy wants to play. The puppy barks, wanting to join in a game.

Farm Kitten climbs up a tree to get away from the puppy. He waits for the puppy to go away.

It has been a busy day, and Farm Kitten is ready for a nap. His senses of sight and smell work together to help him find his way back to the barn.

Now he is sleepy.

Farm Kitten crawls back to his soft bed and falls asleep. He dreams of becoming a true mouser one day.

Butterfly Doctor

Written by Sarah Toast
Illustrated by Mary Lou Faltico

Dr. Butterfly was the busiest bug in town. "I spend so much time at my office," said Dr. Butterfly, "that I don't have much time to play with my own son."

She snapped her fingers. "I know what I'll do. I'll take Billy to work with me."

Billy had always wanted to see where his mom worked. "I can't wait to go to work with you," Billy said, as he packed his favorite stuffed bug.

When Dr. Butterfly and Billy Butterfly arrived at the office, Nurse Nita was busy answering phones.

"Dr. Butterfly's office," Nurse Nita said. "Yes, we can try to fit you in today."

Dr. Butterfly looked at all of the names written in the appointment book. Then Dr. Butterfly looked at the crowded waiting room. It was full of patients.

"Another busy day," she said.

Dr. Butterfly found a place in the waiting room for Billy and his toy bug. "You play here," she told Billy. "I will be back soon."

Dr. Butterfly hurried into the examining room to see her first two patients.

Annie and Archie Ant are twins that needed a checkup for school. Nurse Nita checked Annie's reflexes while Dr. Butterfly weighed and measured Archie.

"You're in perfect health," she told them.

Dr. Butterfly's next patient was Calvin Cricket, the town's mechanic. "I have a terrible headache," said Calvin, "and it won't go away."

"Let me take a look," said Dr. Butterfly. But it did not take her long to figure out what was wrong.

"I have good news and bad news," said Dr. Butterfly. "The good news is you won't need a shot."

"That is good news," said Calvin. "What's the bad news?"

"You have a wrench stuck in your antennae. You won't be able to fix anyone's car until I get it out," said Dr. Butterfly.

"So that's where my wrench went," he said.

Calvin sat on the examining table while Dr. Butterfly untangled the wrench from his antennae. Then Calvin went back to work, and Dr. Butterfly called in her next patient.

"Mom!" called Billy. "I want to show you something."

"In a minute, dear," said Dr. Butterfly. "I'm very busy at the moment."

Dr. Butterfly looked at all the patients she still needed to see. Mr. and Mrs. Dragonfly brought in their baby, Daisy, for her shots. Teddy Termite had chicken pox. Curtis Caterpillar had come down with the flu.

"I'll be with you as soon as I can," Dr. Butterfly told Billy.

"I need your help, too," said Billy.

"I have a waiting room full of patients," Dr. Butterfly said.

Dr. Butterfly took her next patient into her office and closed the door.

Dr. Butterfly gave Daisy Dragonfly her shots. She gave Teddy Termite medicine to make him feel better. She took Curtis Caterpillar's temperature, gave him an aspirin, and told him to get plenty of sleep.

Then Dr. Butterfly rushed over to Billy. "Now, what did you want to show me?" she asked.

"It's my toy bug," said Billy. But before Billy could say anything more, Nurse Nita hurried into the waiting room.

"Dr. Butterfly, come quick," she said. "Sammy Spider fell from his web. I think he broke his leg."

Dr. Butterfly hurried into the examining room to look at Sammy's leg. "It's broken, all right," she said.

Nurse Nita helped Dr. Butterfly put a cast on Sammy's leg. Then Dr. Butterfly and Nurse Nita showed Sammy how to use his crutches.

Nurse Nita and Dr. Butterfly waved good-bye as Sammy hobbled out the door on his crutches. Then she glanced around the waiting room.

"Have we really seen all the patients today?" asked Dr. Butterfly.

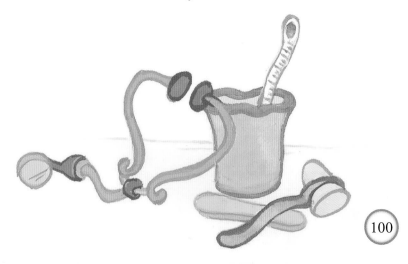

"No, there's one more," said Billy, as he held up his toy bug. One of the bug's seams had torn open and its stuffing was starting to fall out. "Mom, can you fix my toy bug like you fixed all the other bugs?" he asked.

Dr. Butterfly carried Billy's toy bug into the examining room. She took the bug's temperature and listened to its heart. Then she put a bandage over its torn seam.

Billy gave his mother a big hug. "You take very good care of everyone in town," he said. "Especially me."

Baby Kangaroo

Written by Jennifer Boudart
Illustrated by Linda Holt Ayriss

The red gum trees shade the Australian outback on warm afternoons. Kangaroos know this well, so they rest under the trees during the hot summer days.

One kangaroo does not want to take a nap. His name is Joey, and he wants to play.

A kangaroo is called a joey when it is a baby. Joey is only a few months old. Like all kangaroos, he has strong back legs, large feet, and a long tail. When Joey moves, it is easy to see why his legs and body are so big and strong.

He hops! Joey bounces along on his back legs, using his tail for balance. A kangaroo can jump seven feet into the air with one bounce!

Joey finds two other young kangaroos who are awake, too. They start to wrestle with each other.

A clucking noise makes him stop suddenly. It is his mother calling him. She uses the special sound to tell Joey that he has wandered too far from her. Joey quickly returns to his mother.

Joey is very tired after all of his fun and games. He climbs headfirst into a small pouch located in his mother's tummy.

The pouch is the perfect size for her baby. Only Joey's legs are sticking out. Then he turns himself around in the pouch so he can see. A kangaroo mother's pouch makes a great bed for her babies.

Joey knows this pouch very well, because he spends a lot of time there. A joey usually lives in its mother's pouch until it's too big to fit inside—which is about one year.

An adult kangaroo stomps its foot on the ground. That sound means danger! Joey's mother sniffs the air. Suddenly, a pack of dingo dogs comes running from the trees.

The kangaroos must escape! Quickly, they jump away, flying through the air. Joey ducks down into his mother's pouch. His mother has never moved so fast!

Adult kangaroos traveling quickly can cover distances up to 27 feet with each bounce, and they can reach speeds of 40 miles per hour.

Mother Kangaroo jumps fast and far. The pack of dingo dogs cannot keep up. The dingoes drop back. The kangaroos are safe, but they keep on moving. They are heading toward a patch of rain clouds.

The kangaroos know that tasty green grass grows wherever rain has fallen. The group reaches its new home before dark.

A kangaroo's most important senses are smell and hearing. Kangaroos have long ear flaps that they can turn backward and forward to hear sounds from all directions.

The kangaroos settle into their new home. It will soon be night, and it is getting cooler.

Joey's mother nibbles some grass. Joey is still in her pouch. When she stretches down to eat some grass or nibble on leaves, Joey stretches down to eat some grass, too.

Joey's little tummy is now full. He leaves his mother's pouch. Joey hops to a pool filled with fresh rainwater. The pool is new to him. The land where he lives is normally very dry. Joey looks into the water. He sees another kangaroo looking back at him! Who is this strange kangaroo?

Joey leans closer to look in the water at the stranger's face. Oops! Joey dips his nose in the water and gets all wet.

Kangaroos can cool themselves by taking a dip in the water, too. Joey looks around and sees some older kangaroos splashing around in the cool water.

The water feels wonderful. Joey hops right into the cool puddle. Soon other young kangaroos jump in the puddle, too. They discover what the older kangaroos already know—water is fun!

Ziggy's Fine Coat

Written by Catherine McCafferty
Illustrated by Debbie Pinkney

Ziggy was a handsome young tiger cub who lived in the jungle with his parents. His mother was the most kind and beautiful tigress in all of the jungle, and his father was the most handsome tiger. But Ziggy's stripes always made him feel out of place.

One day, Ziggy and his father went to the watering hole for a drink. Ziggy looked at his reflection in the shiny surface of the water.

"Dad, I just don't know what I should do about all these terrible stripes," said Ziggy.

"Son, you have brighter and bolder zigzag stripes than any other cub in the jungle," said his father. "That's why we named you Ziggy."

"Yours and Mama's seem to fit you, but mine just look funny," said Ziggy.

"You'll grow into your stripes one day," said Ziggy's father.

That did not make Ziggy feel better. He thought and thought as he wandered through his jungle home.

"There must be some way to get rid of these stripes," Ziggy muttered to himself.

Just then, Ziggy's parrot friend, Kiko, landed on a flower bush.

"What's the matter, Ziggy?" asked Kiko.

"I don't want to be striped anymore," Ziggy explained.

Kiko hopped out of the big flower bush. "Maybe these bright red flowers could help," suggested Kiko.

Ziggy stared at the beautiful flowers. Suddenly, he came up with an idea.

"Those flower petals just might do the trick!" he said.

Ziggy carefully plucked some of the flower petals from the flower bush.

"This just might work!" Ziggy said.

Ziggy licked his coat and pasted the petals all over himself. Soon all of his black stripes were covered.

"Not a stripe in sight!" said Kiko gleefully.

As Kiko said this, a strong breeze blew through the jungle. The breeze blew all of Ziggy's red flower petals away.

"Oh no," cried Ziggy. "My stripes are back again."

Ziggy's monkey friend, Maka, swung down from a nearby tree. "Why the long face?" asked Maka.

"I'm tired of being striped. I wish I could find a way to get rid of these stripes," said Ziggy.

Maka thought only for a short while. The mischievous monkey was always full of good ideas.

"I have just the thing for you," laughed Maka. "Why don't you paint your stripes with mud?"

Ziggy and Maka ran over to a big mud puddle near the watering hole. "This is just the thing!" said Ziggy.

Ziggy pounced right into the middle of the puddle. Then he rolled around in the soft squishy mud.

"Be sure to get good and muddy!" Maka shouted as he climbed up the tree. "We want to cover up each and every one of those pesky little black stripes with mud!"

"This is going to work," Ziggy said, as he squirmed and wiggled around in the thick mud.

Before long, his stripes were covered with mud.

Ziggy's mother came to the watering hole and saw Ziggy
rolling in the mud. She nudged him over to the water and
scrubbed all the mud off of his coat.

"But Mama," Ziggy complained, "I don't want to be striped
anymore. Don't you ever get tired of being striped?"

"When I was your age, I didn't want to be striped either,"
his mother said. "But then I learned that my coat is special.
Your coat is special, too."

"I guess so," sighed Ziggy, as he hung his head.

Ziggy's mother washed all the mud off him. "Let's play a game," she said. "Close your eyes and count to ten, and then try to find me."

"All right, Mother," sighed Ziggy.

Ziggy had played hide-and-seek before, and he did not see what it had to do with his stripes. But Ziggy counted anyway.

Ziggy looked around for his mother. He looked in the tall grasses. He looked behind a tree and a bush. He could not find her.

"Mother, where are you?" called Ziggy.

"Why, I'm right here, Ziggy," said his mother, stepping out from the tall grasses right in front of him.

"But I didn't see you there at all!" exclaimed Ziggy.

"That's why our stripes are so special," Ziggy's mother told him. "Our orange stripes blend in with the grasses, and our black stripes blend in with the shadows. They make it easy for us to hide."

"My stripes aren't so bad!" Ziggy said. "I'm going to play with Kiko and Maka." He could not wait to show his friends his new trick.

117

Farm Donkey

Written by Catherine McCafferty
Illustrated by Robert Masheris

This is going to be a busy year for Littlefoot! She was born three springs ago, and now she is old enough to help with the farm chores.

When Littlefoot is not working, she is busy playing. She plays with the farmer's children. She likes it when the children chase her. There will always be time for Littlefoot to play, but now she must help the farmer work.

The farmer and his family raise flowers that they sell in their roadside stand. Each morning, the farmer loads freshly cut flowers into baskets that Littlefoot carries on her back. Littlefoot does not mind carrying the flowers. But the farmer minds when Littlefoot tastes them!

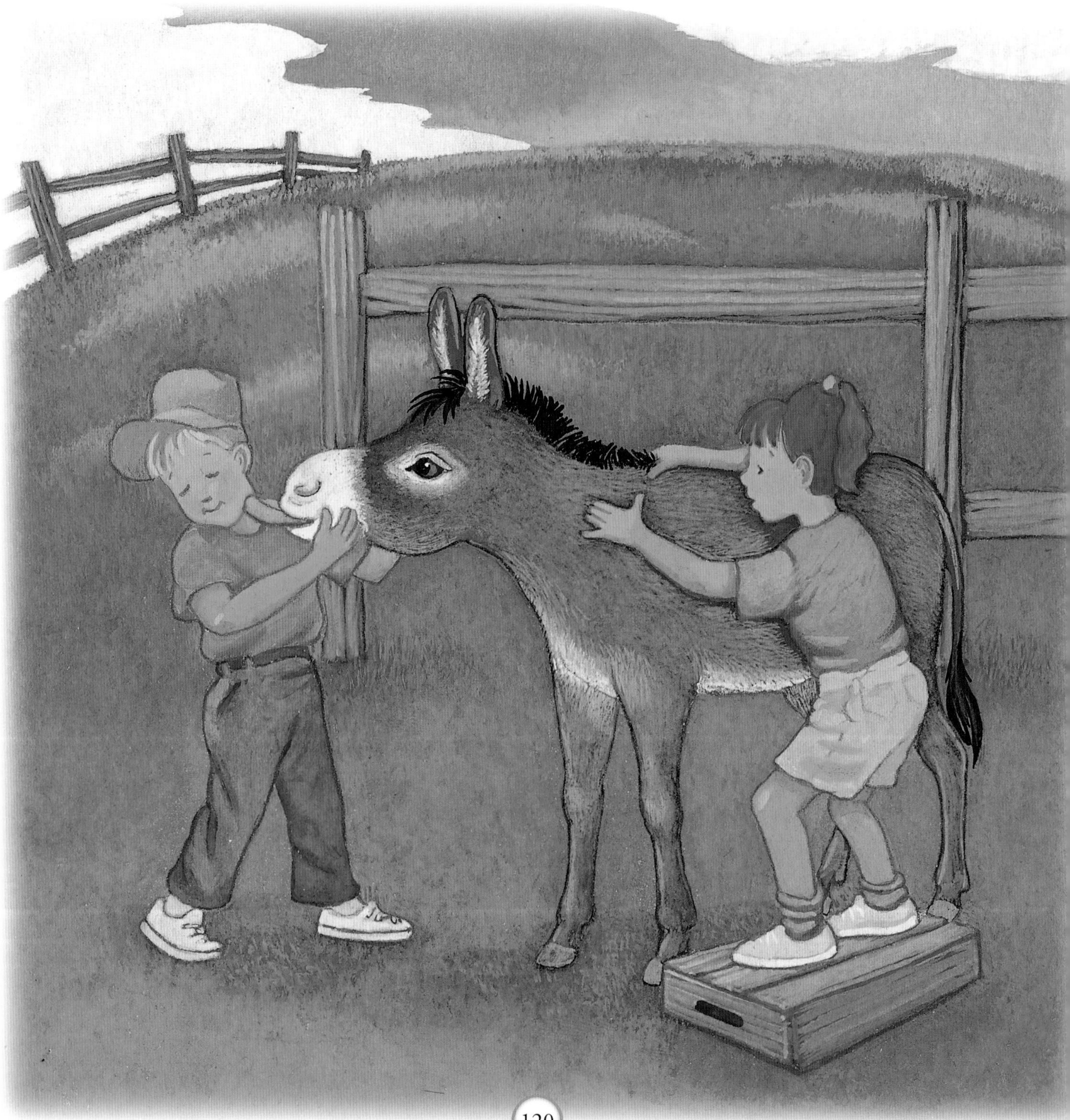

Littlefoot is part of the horse family, but she is different in many ways. Littlefoot is steadier and more patient than most horses. Littlefoot can help the farmer carry things. The farmer can tell Littlefoot is paying attention to him, because she will turn her long ears in the direction of his voice.

Littlefoot's patience and steadiness are very important once summer comes. The farmer sells strawberries now. But instead of carrying them out to the stand, he lets families come and pick the strawberries in his fields.

Many children visit Littlefoot. They pet her, talk to her, and scratch her between her ears.

Sometimes, Littlefoot gives the children rides around the barnyard. Littlefoot loves all the attention and really misses the children when they leave.

In the fall, the children come to see Littlefoot again. The farmer sells pumpkins now. Littlefoot gives hayrides to the children and helps haul pumpkins out to the road for display.

As winter approaches, Littlefoot helps the farmer get ready for the cold weather. She helps bring in the hay. The hay is important for all of the farm animals in the winter. For Littlefoot, the hay will serve as food and bedding.

Once the hay is stored, Littlefoot goes with the farmer into the woods to gather firewood. Littlefoot likes these walks. Littlefoot is very sure-footed on the uneven ground. When the farmer finds a fallen tree, he cuts it into pieces that Littlefoot can haul back to the woodshed. As they walk home, it begins to snow. Littlefoot hurries back to her warm shed.

All night, the snow continues. In the morning, Littlefoot hears the farmer's children laughing. She pokes her head out of the shed and takes one step forward. Her front hoof sinks into the snow. Littlefoot hurries back into the shed.

The farmer's children bring Littlefoot some carrots and try to coax her out into the snow. They want her to give them a sleigh ride. But Littlefoot does not want to walk in the snow.

Farm Donkey

The snow has caused many problems. It has made the roads dangerous for travel.

The farmer's neighbor is out of feed, and he cannot drive to the feed store. The farmer will lend his neighbor some feed. But he needs Littlefoot's help to get there.

The farmer calls to Littlefoot as he walks to her shed. He stamps down the snow in front of the shed for her. When Littlefoot walks out, she does not sink in the packed snow.

The farmer hitches Littlefoot to the sleigh. Walking ahead of her, he stamps down the snow. They move very slowly to the neighbor's house.

Up on the road, the neighbor waits with his horse and cart. Littlefoot has saved the day!

As Littlefoot walks back home she is beginning to get used to the snow. Littlefoot sees the children playing in the snow and trots right over to them. Littlefoot is ready to give them a sleigh ride now!

Cedar's New Tooth

Written by Catherine McCafferty
Illustrated by Jean Pidgeon

Cedar Squirrel sat up in his nest. What got him up so early? Cedar rubbed his eyes and glanced around. His older brothers, Sassafras and Oak, were asleep.

Cedar clapped his paws over his tummy. That is why he woke up! His stomach was growling.

"Maybe I can get a little snack," said Cedar, as he yawned and stretched.

Then Cedar frowned. "Something is different," he said. "Something isn't right."

Cedar glanced around his nest. It did not look different. He peered at his sleeping brothers. They did not look different either.

Then Cedar felt what was different. His front tooth, his very best acorn munching tooth, had fallen out.

"Oh no!" Cedar cried.

Cedar rushed around the nest, scattering leaves and twigs every which way. He looked in every corner and in every nook and cranny. But the tooth was not there.

Cedar even poked his front paw under his sleeping brothers to see if they were sleeping on his tooth. But Cedar did not find it.

"Oak," Cedar whispered. "Please wake up! I can't find my front tooth."

Oak, who was usually so wise, just muttered, "Sassafras probably hid it." Then he rolled over.

Cedar shook his other brother. "Do you know where my tooth is?" But Sassafras continued snoring. Cedar shook him again. "Sassafras!" Cedar whispered.

Sassafras buried his head under the leaves. So Cedar shook even harder. "Sassafras, wake up! Did you take my tooth?"

Sassafras opened one eye. "Why would I want your tooth?" he asked. Cedar shrugged.

"I'll take your acorns," Sassafras mumbled, as he closed his eyes. "You won't be able to crack them with a missing tooth."

No acorns! Sassafras was right. Without that tooth, Cedar would not be able to crack acorns.

"Maybe I just need to practice," said Cedar.

Cedar hurried over to the pile of acorns they had stored for the winter. One of the acorns had rolled away and was in a pile of leaves.

Cedar picked it up. Then he looked at it carefully.

"I'll find a way to crack this," said Cedar. He put the acorn in his mouth.

Cedar bit down, but the acorn did not crack. It just slid out of his mouth.

Cedar tried again and again. But the acorn shell stayed smooth and whole. It did not even crack.

Cedar went to find his mother.

"Mama!" Cedar called out. "Mama, my tooth!"

Cedar ran to her. Then he opened his mouth wide so his mother could see.

"It looks like you've lost one," said his mother. She did not seem worried.

"But I can't eat acorns without my tooth," said Cedar.

His mother smiled. "Maybe you can't now. But you'll grow a new tooth soon."

"How will I crack acorns until then?" asked Cedar.

His mother chuckled. "You'll have to eat something else for a while."

At breakfast, Cedar's mouth watered as he looked at the acorns and nuts Oak and Sassafras ate. Cedar had a pile of mushy berries.

"I won't wait to get my new tooth," said Cedar. "I'm going to get one now."

"Where do you think you'll find another squirrel tooth?" asked Sassafras.

"I don't know," said Cedar.

Cedar left his berries and raced through the woods to find his friend, Buck Deer.

"Buck," Cedar said, "my tooth fell out." He crawled up on Buck's antlers and opened his mouth wide. "Do you know where I can get a new one?"

Buck peered into Cedar's mouth. "There's only one place to get a new squirrel tooth," he said.

Cedar's eyes widened. "Where?"

Buck chuckled. "Inside a squirrel's mouth, of course."

Cedar hung his head and stared at the ground. "Don't be funny," he said.

"A new tooth will grow," Buck said

"I know," said Cedar. "But I don't want to wait that long before I can eat acorns again."

Buck looked into Cedar's mouth again. "You won't have to," he said. "Your new one is already coming in."

Cedar felt the spot where his tooth used to be. "You're right!" Cedar said. "I'm getting a new tooth!"

"You'll be cracking acorns again soon," Buck said.

"I will get used to eating berries for just a little while." Cedar said.

He waved good-bye to Buck and ran home to have his breakfast.

Panda Baby

Written by Sarah Toast
Illustrated by Debbie Pinkney

It is late in the summer in the steep and rocky mountains of China. In the mist of twilight, Mother Panda stirs.

Mother Panda leaves her den to climb farther down the side of the mountain. She will eat bamboo all night.

Mother Panda has an extra "thumb" that helps her handle the bamboo leaves, stems, and shoots with great care. Mother Panda spends most of her time eating the tough bamboo.

Panda bears are not able to digest bamboo very well, so they must eat up to sixty pounds of bamboo a day to get the energy they need.

To find this much bamboo, Mother Panda roams all over looking for good feeding places.

Pandas do not have much free time, because they spend so much time eating all of this bamboo.

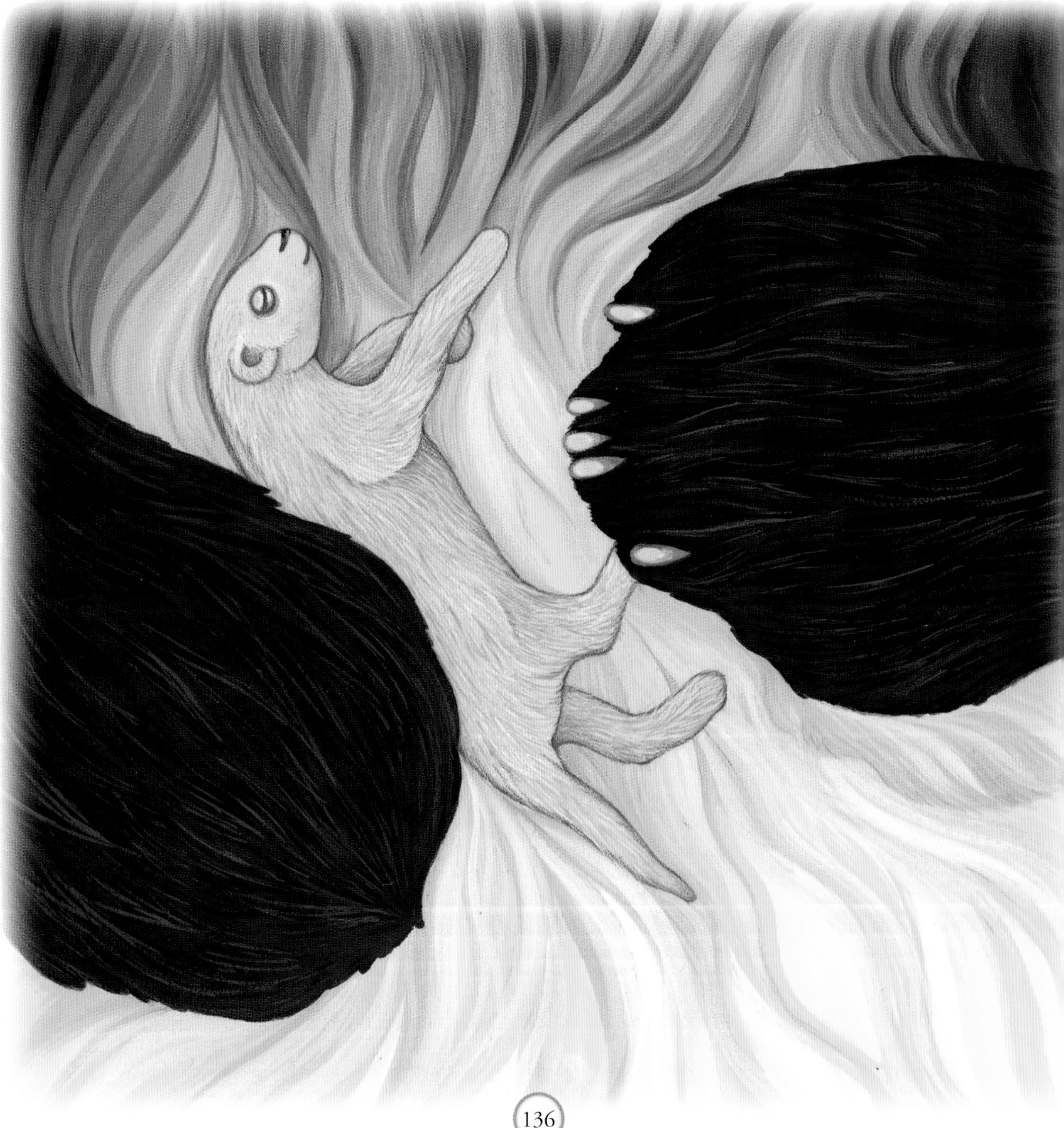

In the gray dawn, Mother Panda climbs back up the side of the mountain and enters her cave. There she gives birth to her tiny baby.

Panda Baby is pink, with only a small amount of fur. His eyes are closed, but he has a loud squeal. A baby panda is very small when it is born. It weighs only five ounces and could be held in a human's hand!

Mother Panda cradles Panda Baby against her chest with her large forepaws. She has a lot to do now that Panda Baby has arrived.

Mother Panda stays inside the warm den with her baby. She nurses Panda Baby, but for several days she does not go out to find food for herself. Mother Panda loves her helpless little panda cub. A mother panda cradles her cub constantly for the first month of its life.

In only a month, Panda Baby has the same warm fur coat as his mother. Not long after that, his eyes open. From then on, Mother Panda can take her cub out of the den.

Mother Panda will carry her baby with her everywhere she goes for a long time. Mother Panda can carry her cub using her mouth. She gently picks the baby up and is very careful to make sure that little Panda Baby will not fall.

It is late in the autumn when Panda Baby learns to stand up. In early winter, Panda Baby is finally able to run and play.

Mother Panda and Panda Baby roam the bamboo groves to find enough food for the hungry mother. Panda Baby plays in the leaves while his mother eats. He is not old enough to eat bamboo yet.

Then they search for a comfortable place to rest. They like to sleep in trees, caves, and other rocky places.

Soon after its first birthday, a young panda will leave its mother to find its own territory and its own bamboo supply.

When Panda Baby is older, he will spend most of his life alone in a small territory. A panda marks its territory by rubbing the scent glands near its back legs against trees. Sometimes a panda marks a tree while standing on its head!

But for now, Baby Panda will spend all his time with Mother Panda. They climb down the mountain as the winter gets colder. They will not sleep through the winter like some bears do.

Bamboo stays green all year round, so Mother Panda will be able to find plenty to eat during the winter. Mother Panda will continue to nurse Panda Baby for many more months.

In winter, the bamboo forests are covered in snow, but pandas do not mind. Their large, round bodies keep in the heat, and their thick fur coats keep them dry.

The first snow of winter will soon fall. After a day of playing and exploring, Panda Baby rests in his den. He snuggles up to his mother and enjoys a nice long nap.

Speedy Colt

Written by Catherine McCafferty
Illustrated by Erin Mauterer

Speedy was a lively colt. He lived on a farm with many horses. Speedy's whole family lived there and so did other families with their little colts.

Speedy and his friends were born in the early spring. They enjoyed their very first summer together. The colts had nothing much to do but play all day in the fields.

Speedy had a best friend named Lightning. Speedy and Lightning were growing bigger and stronger every day.

"Come on, Lightning!" said Speedy. "Let's play chase with the others."

All the colts tore around the fields. They chased each other, the butterflies, and the wind. They all loved to play chase together.

Speedy and Lightning were the fastest colts on the farm. They raced way ahead of the other colts. Then they circled back to their friends and played chase with them some more.

One day, Speedy's mother said to him, "I am glad to see you are growing into a big strong colt."

"My best friend Lightning is as fast as I am!" Speedy told his mother.

Speedy started to race off toward the field where Lightning was waiting for him to play. But his mother called after him.

"Not so fast, Speedy," said his mother. "I have something important to talk to you about."

Speedy came back to his mother. "Sorry, Mother," he said. Speedy waited to hear what she had to say.

"Son," said his mother, "your grandfather would like to spend some time with you tomorrow. He wants to show you around the woods behind the big field."

"But Mom," said Speedy, "Grandpa is so slow! He doesn't play chase, and he can't race! He's not much fun."

"Your grandfather may be a little slower than your friends, but that doesn't mean he isn't fun," said Speedy's mother. "And he would enjoy your company."

"I really love Grandpa," said Speedy. "I want him to be happy. I promise I'll visit with him tomorrow."

"That would be very nice, Speedy," said his mother. "Have fun playing with your friends today."

Speedy ran off to the field. Lightning and the other colts were waiting for him there.

First, they played chase. Then Speedy and Lightning raced each other. Speedy won the first race, and Lightning won the second one.

The next day, Speedy forgot all about his promise to his mother. He and his friends played all day without a care, until Speedy and Lightning's big race.

Speedy and Lightning raced each other like they always did. But this time, they ran clear to the edge of the field, which is where the woods began.

Speedy remembered that his grandfather wanted to show him the woods. "I will keep my promise tomorrow!" Speedy thought to himself. "Today, I'll explore the woods with Lightning." But Lightning did not want to go any farther.

"Then I'll go on my own," Speedy said, as he trotted off.

"Come back," Lightning called. "You'll get lost!"

"No I won't," shouted Speedy. "Don't worry about me."

At first, Speedy whinnied with joy as he trotted farther and farther into the woods. But he ran so fast that he did not remember which way he had come.

One wide path joined another. Speedy was not sure which way to turn to get back to the field. First, he tried one path, then he tried another. No matter which way he tried, he was still in the woods.

Speedy stood still and tried not to cry. He did not know when he would see his mother and his grandfather again.

"They must be very worried," Speedy thought to himself. As he hung his head down, a tear ran down his cheek and fell onto the path below.

Just then Speedy heard the steady clip-clop of a horse walking down the path. He looked up and was instantly filled with relief. It was his grandfather walking toward him!

"Grandpa!" said Speedy. "I was lost, but you found me!"

"Lightning told me you never came out of the woods," his grandfather said.

"Why aren't you lost, too?" asked Speedy.

"I know every path on the farm and in these woods," said his grandfather, as they walked out together. "I've spent years on these paths. I can take you and Lightning on a long walk through the woods tomorrow."

"That's great!" said Speedy. "I guess there's more to life than running around."

"Speedy," his grandfather said, "sometimes it's nice just to slow down a little."

Elly's Little Friend

Written by Catherine McCafferty
Illustrated by Debbie Pinkney

Elly thundered through the grass to find her mother. "Mama!" she called out, "I have a new friend!"

Elly was very proud of her news. She was the youngest elephant in her family, and she did not do things by herself very often.

"I knew you could make friends if you tried," she said. "Tell me all about this new pal of yours."

"Her name is Mindy," said Elly. "She's smart and she's funny. We met under the shady tree. That's my favorite spot to play. It's Mindy's favorite spot, too. As soon as we started talking, we knew we would be friends."

"Well, it sounds like you are a lot alike," said Elly's mother.

"We are!" said Elly.

"Invite Mindy for dinner," said her mother, "then our whole family can meet her."

Elly ran to the shady tree to tell Mindy the good news.

"You'll really like eating dinner with us," Elly told her new best friend.

"I hope your family likes me," said Mindy.

"They'll love you," said Elly.

Mindy scrambled up onto Elly's trunk. Then the two friends went to meet Elly's family for dinner.

Elly's mother and sisters did not see Mindy at first. "Mama," Elly said, as she lifted her trunk, "this is Mindy."

"A mouse!" shouted Elly's sister. Elly's family stomped, thundered, and trumpeted away from Mindy.

Mindy watched Elly's family leave. "They didn't like me at all," she squeaked softly.

Elly smiled. "They barely met you," she said. "Once they know you, I'm sure they'll like you as much as I do."

"Maybe you should come to my house," said Mindy.

Mindy and Elly set out over the grass. But it was worse at Mindy's house. Her family heard Elly's heavy footsteps coming and scampered away.

"Your family doesn't like me, either," said Elly.

"How can they not like you?" said Mindy. "They didn't even meet you. I don't understand." Mindy shook her tiny head sadly.

"That's it, Mindy!" said Elly. "I'll tell my mama and my sisters to just talk to you. Then they'll love you."

"I'll tell my family the same thing," said Mindy.

As Mindy left to tell her family, Elly went to talk to her mother and sisters. She found them by the watering hole.

"Mama, if you'd just give Mindy a chance," said Elly, "you'd like her. I know you would."

"I'm sorry, Elly," said her mother, "but elephants have never liked mice."

Elly found Mindy back at the shady tree.

"It's no use," said Mindy. "My family is afraid of you. They think you'll trample us."

"I wouldn't," cried Elly.

"I would never hurt your family, either," cried Mindy.

Elly's mother saw Elly crying. She ran to dry off her daughter's tears with a large leaf.

Mindy's mother saw Mindy crying, too. She ran to wipe Mindy's face with a tiny leaf.

The two mothers stopped to look at each other. "Maybe our families are alike after all," said Elly's mother.

"Elly and Mindy would be sad if we separated them," said Mindy's mother.

Elly's mother nodded. "We should try to get along."

Soon Mindy's family got an elephant's view of the world. And Elly's family learned to enjoy all the little things in life.

The End